CONTENTS

PEOPLE YOU WILL MEET 4

STORY #1:
TAG TEAM 6

STORY #2:
TECH WRECK 22

STORY #3:
THE ANCIENT LIBRARY
OF HONOMIZU 38

PEOPLE YOU WILL MEET

NYA:
Ninja and Master of Water.

KAI:
Ninja and Master of Fire.

KRUX:
One of the Time Twins.
He is a villain with power
over time.

BRICK ADVENTURES
3 NEW ACTION-PACKED, ILLUSTRATED STORIES!

BROTHER/SISTER SQUAD

By Meredith Rusu

SCHOLASTIC INC.

Published by Scholastic Inc., *Publishers since 1920*. SCHOLASTIC and associated logos are trademarks and/or registered trademarks of Scholastic Inc.

The publisher does not have any control over and does not assume any responsibility for author or third-party websites or their content.

This book is a work of fiction. Names, characters, places, and incidents are either the product of the author's imagination or are used fictitiously, and any resemblance to actual persons, living or dead, business establishments, events, or locales is entirely coincidental.

ISBN 978-1-338-17380-2

10 9 8 7 6 5 4 3 2 1   18 19 20 21 22

Printed in the U.S.A.   40
First printing 2018

ACRONIX:
Krux's twin. He is also a villain with power over time.

VERMILLION WARRIORS:
Soldiers that serve Krux and Acronix. Their bodies are made of tiny snakes.

MAYA:
Kai and Nya's mother.

RAY:
Kai and Nya's father.

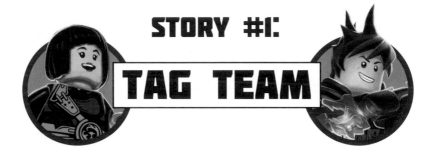

STORY #1:

TAG TEAM

"**R**ight, we're on our way!"

Nya switched off the **Ultra Stealth Raider**'s communicator. Then she and her brother, **Kai**, zoomed through the empty streets of Ninjago City.

"The gang is back at the cave," Nya said. "We're going to meet them there."

It was evening. Nya and Kai had just escaped from a fight with **Krux** and **Acronix**, the **Time Twins**. Meanwhile, the other ninja had been fighting snake warriors. The snakes were trying to kidnap the best workers in the land.

One thing was clear: Krux and Acronix had not been defeated in their battle against the **Elemental Masters** forty years ago. They were back, and they had an evil plan — and an army of snake warriors!

VRRRRMMMM!

"I don't get it," Kai said. "Why are Krux and Acronix getting snakes to kidnap people? What's their big plan?"

Nya frowned. "I don't know. But it's up to us to find out."

Kai looked at the samurai helmet in his hands. He'd taken it from a snake warrior during the battle. Kai had discovered it was the same as the helmets worn by Krux and Acronix during their battle against the Elemental Masters long ago.

Kai and Nya's parents had been at that battle, helping Master Wu defeat the Time Twins. Or so Kai had thought.

Krux had told Kai something disturbing.

"Your parents didn't fight against us," he'd sneered. "They fought *with* us! Your parents were traitors!"

Now Kai wasn't sure what to think. What if their parents had been traitors? It would mean everything he believed was a lie. Even worse . . . how would he tell Nya?

"You okay, bro?" Nya asked Kai. "You seem down."

Kai nodded. "I'm okay. It's just — look out!"

Kai pointed up ahead. A legion of snake warriors was blocking their way!

"Hang on!" Nya yelled. She swerved sharply to the right.

But the snakes were clever. Two of them grabbed on to the Ultra Stealth Raider. They began climbing up the sides!

"Oh, no, you don't!" Nya said. She used the blaster to zap a warrior off the vehicle. "No free rides!"

"Yeah." Kai blasted the other with a fireball. "We're too hot for you to handle!"

TOO HOT TO HANDLE!

Kai guarded Nya's back as she steered. Meanwhile, the two warriors crashed onto the street below and smashed apart into dozens of snakes.

Soon the snakes regrouped and slithered back into their armor. They re-formed into complete warriors and started chasing the Ultra Stealth Raider again. Twenty more warriors followed them.

HANDS OFF MY RIDE!

These enemies were fast. They began leaping up onto the Ultra Stealth Raider and pulling off pieces!

"Hey, I just had this shined and cleaned!" Nya cried, annoyed. She blasted several warriors with her water power, and they tumbled off.

"Kai," Nya said urgently. "There are too many of them. I can't steer if they're pulling our ride apart. We need to get them off for good."

"I know," Kai said. He used a flaming **Spinjitzu** attack on a warrior who'd dropped down from above. "But how? There are twenty of them and only two of us —"

The helmet suddenly rolled off Kai's lap to the floor. He stared at it for a moment, lost in thought.

Just like there were only two of our parents, Kai thought. Two friends of the Elemental Masters . . . or two traitors?

"Kai!" Nya cried as a snake warrior grabbed her arm. "Uunngh!" She blasted the warrior apart with water power. "What's with you? I need your help to battle these snakes!"

"Sorry." Kai shook his head. "I got — distracted."

"We have to work together," Nya insisted. "It's the only way to defeat them."

Nya was right. Kai couldn't worry about the past. His sister needed him!

Suddenly, Kai had an idea. "Nya — the only way to stop them is to keep them from getting back in their armor. Remember how I said this ride was 'too hot for them to handle'? What if we literally make it too hot?"

Nya smiled. "I like the sound of that! And I know just the trick."

She slammed on the brakes, and the Ultra Stealth Raider skidded to a halt next to a fire hydrant.

Kai and Nya waited until all the snake warriors had climbed onto the vehicle. Then they pulled on their hoods.

The snakes began pulling at the metal covering the Ultra Stealth Raider. And then . . .

"Now!" cried Kai.

Kai blasted each snake warrior with fire. As each one shattered, Nya used water from the fire hydrant to round up their armor.

Kai blasted the last snakes from their armor. Then he aimed a blast of fire at the water. It bubbled and boiled, creating a fiery moat around the Ultra Stealth Raider. The enemies' armor floated on the water's surface.

YOU'RE IN HOT WATER NOW!

The scattered snakes tried to slide back, but —

"Hisssssssssssssssssssss!" The snakes got burned by the boiling water. It was too hot for them. They couldn't reach their armor!

Defeated, the snakes slithered away.

At last, Kai and Nya were safe. Kai's plan had worked!

"That was a great idea," said Nya, patting Kai on the back. "Thanks for being there for me."

Kai grinned. "You can count on me, sis. That's what family is for."

STORY #2:

TECH WRECK

Deep below the streets of Ninjago City, a strange army was marching through underground tunnels. A group of snakes known as **Vermillion Warriors** pushed along their prisoners — citizens of Ninjago City. More snakes slithered and hissed beside them. The group was led by two evil brothers: Krux and Acronix, the Time Twins.

So far, the brothers' plan was going well. They had captured the best builders from all over the city. Up on the surface, Vermillion Warriors were stealing all the metal in the city.

The brothers and their prisoners would soon reach the secret swamp land base, where thousands of snakes were about to hatch.

Now the Time Twins had enough metal to create armor for the newborn snakes. And they had Ninjago's best workers to forge it. Soon they would have an invincible army! Then they could defeat Master Wu and the Elemental Masters.

That was, if they could find their way through the tunnels.

"Let me get this straight, brother," Acronix said, annoyed. "We are about to construct the strongest army in history, but we're lost in the tunnels leading to that army?"

"We're not lost," Krux snapped. "Give me a minute; I'll remember the way."

"This would be easier if you would use technology," Acronix said. "My **BorgPad** has a bunch of apps that could help."

Krux snarled. If there was one thing he hated more than anything in the world, it was technology.

"Modern technology has done nothing but drain away what little intelligence these goofballs had to begin with," he said huffily.

"But, brother, you have to admit this is cool." Acronix pulled out his BorgPad. "It has an app for **sonar navigation** and a FLASHLIGHT!"

Acronix shone the BorgPad's flashlight in Krux's eyes. Angrily, Krux knocked it aside. "You will never convince me," he said. "The old ways are still the best."

But at that moment, Krux led the army straight into . . . another dead end. They would have to turn back.

"The best for getting lost." Acronix smirked. "Here, let me show you how technology can solve this problem."

With a few quick swipes, Acronix brought up the sonar navigation app on his BorgPad. It made a pinging sound, pointing the troops in the right direction.

"You see, brother?" Acronix said smugly. "Technology at your service."

Reluctantly, Krux allowed Acronix to lead the way.

But suddenly, the app began to glitch.
BRRRRZZZZ!

The BorgPad began to sound a shrill alarm.
Krux, Acronix, the army, and all the prisoners
covered their ears.

"Hang on," said Acronix, swiping the pad's
screen. But it was locked, and the alarm
continued. "Argh," he said. "The app must
have frozen. If I can just get back to the home
screen . . ."

Acronix shook the pad. But he lost his grip,
and the pad went flying into the Vermillion
Warrior directly next to them! SMASH!

The warrior's armor shattered, sending snakes flying everywhere. Krux and Acronix turned just in time to see the BorgPad lying on the ground.

"Oh, no!" Acronix cried, racing back. "Is it . . . is it . . ."

He picked up the BorgPad and stroked it. "Phew." He sighed. "Not cracked. Just a little ding on the side. My BorgCare plan should cover it."

SMASH!

Meanwhile, the snakes from the smashed Vermillion Warrior slithered back into the armor and became whole again.

"Your troops seem to be falling apart," Acronix told his brother.

"They are sick of your love of silly technology," Krux replied. "I will show you once and for all how the old ways are the best."

With pride, Krux pulled a big compass out of his pocket.

"Really, brother? A compass?" asked Acronix.

"It'll get the job done," Krux said. "Better than your silly sonar app. Follow me."

Once again, Krux took the lead. The troops walked for a long time, heading around and around and around the tunnels.

"Hmmm," Krux said thoughtfully. "I don't remember the base being this far away."

"It feels like we've been walking in circles," said Acronix.

"We are walking in circles," one of their prisoners suddenly piped up.

The brothers turned slowly to look at the man. It was a construction worker in a hard hat.

REALLY? A COMPASS??

"Mined these tunnels all my life," the worker continued. "The ground beneath Ninjago City is rich in magnetic ore. And I'm pretty sure that magnetic ore is messing with that there old-timey compass."

"Not again!" Acronix said angrily. "Brother, you have been leading us in circles!"

Acronix flung his Time Blade aside. It slammed hard into the same Vermillion Warrior as before. Once again, snakes went flying.

"We are wasting time," Acronix snapped. "And I hate wasting . . ." He glanced down as a snake slithered past his foot and back into the armor. "Time."

Acronix picked up the Time Blade. "We are doing this all wrong. Let us combine old and new. We can use your compass and the magnetic feature of my BorgWatch."

Krux blinked. "That pesky watch has such a device?"

Acronix nodded. "I read about it in the owner's manual. It will help your compass work properly. Old and new. And then, perhaps we shall reach the base."

Krux watched as Acronix pulled up the app on his BorgWatch. Acronix pressed a button . . .

And suddenly, the watch created a huge sonic boom! The brothers stumbled back as the sound wave slammed into the same Vermillion Warrior. His snakes and armor went flying.

"What in time was that?" Krux asked, dazed.

"Hmmm." Acronix shook his head. "Perhaps the app only works aboveground." He looked up and spotted a mark at the top of the tunnel wall. "Brother, do you see that?"

Krux smiled. "Ah, yes! I forgot about the markings. I made them years ago to help guide us on our way. That arrow points to the tunnel that leads to the base."

Acronix frowned. "How could you forget that?"

Krux shrugged. "Forty years is a long time, brother. Now we can continue without the use of your silly technology."

Acronix sighed. Then he spied the dizzy, confused snakes from the shattered Vermillion Warrior slithering back into their armor.

"I doubt we will ever agree on technology versus the old ways," he said. "But I'm certain we can agree on one thing. Your generals must teach this warrior to control himself. He keeps falling apart."

The warrior was dumbfounded. He looked back and forth between the brothers in shock.

"Indeed," Krux nodded. "That is one thing we can agree on."

STORY #3:

THE ANCIENT LIBRARY OF HONOMIZU

Thunder rumbled in the black sky as the *Destiny's Bounty* flew high above the Boiling Sea. Steam rose from the glowing red water. Lightning flashed. Even the bravest warrior would shiver at the sight.

NOT EXACTLY OUR IDEAL VACATION SPOT...

But Kai and Nya gazed out over the bow of the *Destiny's Bounty*. Kai held the **Synthesword**. Nya carried the glowing red **Reversal Blade**.

Kai and Nya's parents, **Ray** and **Maya**, joined the ninja.

"Gotta say," Kai said, chuckling, "this isn't the spot I would've chosen for our first family vacation."

"Me either, son," said Ray. "We'll choose the next place together. I promise."

Kai and Nya smiled. Not long ago, they had believed their parents were dead, and that they were orphans. But then they'd learned that their mother and father were alive. The Time Twins had held Ray and Maya captive for years.

Now that Krux and Acronix were defeated, it was up to Kai and Nya to do as their parents had done so many years before. They had to return the Reversal Blade to the **Library of Honomizu** deep beneath the Boiling Sea. Only the Elemental Masters of Fire and Water could make the journey. The powerful Reversal Blade would be safe there.

Ray and Maya had passed their powers on to Kai and Nya, so it was up to them to return the Reversal Blade.

"I am sorry you two must go back down there," Maya said, worried.

"We'll be fine, Mom," Nya said. "We've done it before. And this time we'll have you to guide us."

Maya frowned. "What do you mean? You know we can't make the journey with you."

Nya pulled out two devices. "Before we left, I made a little gadget to help us. This **communicator** will work underwater — even boiling water. We'll take one, and you and Dad take the other. That way, we'll be able to talk to you during our journey."

Maya smiled proudly. "When did my little girl get so smart?"

"It must run in the family." Nya grinned. "You ready, bro?"

"You know it, sis," Kai replied.

Kai began twirling the Synthesword above his head. The blade was the key to creating the **Fusion Dragon**, the only creature capable of surviving in the Boiling Sea.

Nya blasted the Synthesword with water; Kai blasted it with fire.

A moment later, the majestic two-headed Fusion Dragon appeared! Kai and Nya hopped aboard.

"Be careful, children!" cried Maya. "Remember to work together!"

"We will, Mom!" Kai shouted. Then the Boiling Sea parted for the Fusion Dragon. Kai and Nya dived into the depths.

The Fusion Dragon sped through the raging water. Finally, they reached a narrow passage far below the surface.

Quickly, Kai and Nya absorbed the Fusion Dragon back into the Synthesword. Each took a deep breath, and together they swam through the passage.

Kai and Nya emerged into an enormous cavern. Nya formed a water slide down the passages that led to the bottom.

Brother and sister slid down to the spot where the Library of Honomizu rested on the ocean floor.

Kai and Nya stood before the broken iron door of the library.

"Whew!" Nya exclaimed. "That was a wild trip, even the second time around!"

"Mom? Dad?" Kai spoke into the communicator. "Can you hear me?"

"We can." Their mother's voice sounded funny over the speaker. "Are you safe?"

"Yes," said Nya. "We're at the door to the library."

WHEW! WHAT A WILD RIDE!

"But it's wrecked," Kai said.

"Did something destroy the iron door I forged?" Ray asked.

"Uh, not exactly," said Kai.

"The last time we were down here, Kai grabbed the Reversal Blade before I could take hold of it, too," Nya said. "That made the library door collapse."

"You must always work together," Maya reminded them.

"We know," Kai said. "I was anxious last time, that's all."

"He was hotheaded," Nya said.

Kai shot her a look. "At least there aren't any **Geotomic Rock Monsters** around," he said.

The last time Kai and Nya had been here, creatures called Geotomic Rock Monsters had guarded the entrance to the library. Kai and Nya had combined their powers to create steam that blasted the creatures apart. Now there was no sign of them.

"You'll need to reforge the door," Kai's father instructed. "And to learn that, you'll need a book stored in the library. It's covered in dark red leather. If you find it, I can guide you to reforge the door stronger than before."

"You got it, Dad," said Kai.

Carefully, the two ninja stepped into the enormous library. Thousands of books lined the shelves.

"Where would the book be, Dad?" Kai asked.

"Behind the stand where the Reversal Blade should be placed," Ray replied.

Suddenly, Kai and Nya could hear Maya's voice again. "Children, it's me. Did I hear you say there were no Geotomic Rock Monsters?"

Nya nodded. "Yeah, Mom. We must have scared them off pretty well last time. It's quiet here now."

"Be careful," warned Maya. "It's odd for the rock monsters to leave their guard post."

Kai and Nya began scanning the shelves for a large book covered in red leather.

"I don't see it, Dad," said Kai. "Are you sure it's here?"

"It should be," Ray's voice came over the speaker. "That's where I left it all those years ago."

"Wait, there it is!" Nya exclaimed, pointing to a high shelf. "See? On the other side of the library. The book glowing red. That must be it!"

"Glowing red?" Maya asked.

Kai and Nya bounded over to the shelf and began climbing up a ladder to reach the book.

"Kids, listen to me," said Ray. "No one could have moved that book from where I left it. Because no one other than the Masters of Fire and Water can survive beneath the Boiling Sea."

"Except . . ." said Maya's voice.

"Except who?" Nya asked.

At that moment, they realized something was very, very wrong.

As soon as Kai pulled the book from the shelf, the empty space glowed fiery red. The gaps between the books began to glow. Something was behind the shelf. And it was growing stronger.

"Uh, Mom, Dad." Nya and Kai raced across the room. "I think we found the Geotomic Rock Monsters."

CRASH!

Books went flying. The shelves cracked apart. An enormous creature stepped through!

"Whoa!" Kai yelled. "I don't remember these rock baddies being so — BIG!"

"Kids, what's happening?" Ray called through the communicator.

"Can't talk, Dad!" Nya and Kai leaped out of the way as the fearsome creature aimed a lava blast at them. "Very angry rock monster attacking!"

CRASH!

The creature howled and fired another blast at Kai and Nya. The ninja barely managed to dodge out of the way.

"And I thought the first ones were bad," Kai said to Nya. "Turns out, they were just babies!"

"The only way to beat it is to work together," Nya said. "We have to steam-blast it from the inside like before. Ready?"

"As ever, sis," said Kai. "One — two — THREE!"

Together, Nya pummeled the rock monster with water blasts while Kai heated the water up to steam.

AHHH!

The water hissed and crackled as it hit the creature. For a moment, it looked like it would burst! And then —

"ROAR!!!!" The monster turned all the steam into a fiery blast. It aimed right at Kai and Nya!

"AHHH!" the ninja cried.

Nya quickly created a water-bubble shield around her and Kai. It took all her energy, but the shield held. Barely.

"Rocky's learned a new trick!" Kai cried.

"How do we beat him?" Nya asked. "If working together isn't the answer, what is?"

"Kids!" Their mother's voice crackled over the communicator. "You need to work together, now more than ever!"

"But how?" Nya yelled as another blast almost hit them.

"The Synthesword," Ray insisted. "Use it now!"

Kai and Nya looked at each other.

"The dragon?" Kai asked. "Do you think . . . ?"

"It's worth a shot," said Nya. "Let's go!"

Kai raised the sword, and he and Nya shot the blade with water and fire.

RUMMMMMMMMMBLE.

With a great SMASH, the Fusion Dragon appeared.

"Now's our chance!" shouted Nya. "Let's show Rocky here some REAL fire power!"

"*NINJA-GO!*" Using all their strength, Kai and Nya infused the dragon with their fire and water powers. They could feel the dragon rumbling the ground beneath them. And then — *FWOOM!*

The dragon unleashed a fiery blast like nothing Kai and Nya had ever seen. The Geotomic Rock Monster howled in surprise. It started to crack apart.

With a furious roar, the monster bounded away. It stumbled through the broken iron door and into the depths of the Boiling Sea.

"We did it!" Kai and Nya sighed.

"Kids, are you all right?" Maya asked.

"Yeah, Mom," said Nya. "You were right. Working together was the key."

"And I got the book, Dad," said Kai. "Ready to get to work?"

Several hours later, the new iron door to the Library of Honomizu stood proud and tall. It was stronger than ever.

Kai and Nya carefully replaced the Reversal Blade on its base. Then they sealed the door shut and began the long journey back to the Boiling Sea's surface.

FWOOM!

Soon Kai and Nya were standing aboard the *Destiny's Bounty*, hugging their parents.

"Great work, kids," Ray said, beaming.

"We're so proud of you both," Maya added.

"Thanks," Nya said, smiling. "But we couldn't have done it without you. I'd say today's work has earned us all some time off. What do you say we start that family vacation? After all, we have a lot of time to make up for."

LET'S CHILL OUT FOR A CHANGE!

"I think that's an excellent idea," said Ray. "Where would you like to go?"

"Anywhere, as long as we're together," said Kai. Then he winked. "Let's choose somewhere we can chill out for a change."

GLOSSARY

BorgPad: A small, computer-like device invented by Cyrus Borg, a famous inventor.

communicator: A tiny device that allows two people to speak to each other from a distance.

Destiny's Bounty: A flying ship that the ninja use as a base.

Elemental Masters: Kai and Nya are Elemental Masters — ninja with powers over the elements, like fire and water.

Fusion Dragon: A powerful dragon that can dive into the Boiling Sea.

Geotomic Rock Monster: An enormous monster made of rock and lava.

Library of Honomizu: An ancient library buried under the Boiling Sea.

Reversal Blade: A sword with the power to turn back time.

sonar navigation: A way of finding your way around using sound waves.

Spinjitzu: A martial art used to defeat the forces of evil. Kai and Nya are both Masters of Spinjitzu.

Synthesword: A special weapon that unites the powers of fire and water to create the Fusion Dragon.

Ultra Stealth Raider: A superfast vehicle the ninja use